ETERNUS

Adeo

TESSA RICE

COPYRIGHT INFORMATION

ETERNUS

Adeo

www.KahunaResearchGroup.org/books

ISBN: 979-8-9859293-0-0 (soft cover)

First U.S. Edition: March 2022

Published by KRG Publishing; an imprint of Kahuna Research Group – Hawaii's premier paranormal research organization & independent publishing company. Our books may be purchased in bulk for promotional, educational or commercial use.

KRG PUBLISHING
An imprint of Kahuna Research Group

10 9 8 7 6 5 4 3 2 1

Also from KRG Publishing

Maui Vortex Field Guide
(Zach Royer, 2019. Also available as a Kindle eBook.)

Apocalyptic Revelations: The Emergence of Earth's Spiritual Awakening
(Sean McCleary, 2019)

Metaphysical Revelations: Information on the Dawning of a New Age
(Sean McCleary, 2018)

Hawai'i Vortex Field Guide
(Zach Royer, 2014. Also available as a Kindle eBook.)

Pyramid Rising: Planetary Acupuncture to Combat Climate Change
(Zach Royer, 2012)

TESSA RICE

CONTENTS

CHAPTER ONE

The United States, 2300 A.D.

I closed my eyes, breathed in the smell of the lilacs, my arms crossed behind my head. How cruel that such a beautiful day in The Grove had to be spent alone.

The Grove, which was really an abandoned neighborhood overgrown with foliage, was also closest to Everest Town, where Davan Hier was now living. I had almost invited him out with me, but I knew I had to come by myself. I thought of Jerad Peters, my best friend since second grade, if he was a girl, maybe...

At this thought, I ripped up a clump of grass and flung it as hard as I could. If it weren't for those stupid Moral Laws, if it weren't for the Council...the branches rustled at my sudden outburst and electricity crackled in my fingers. I drew a sharp breath, forcing myself to calm down. Having the power to manipulate the four elements of industry didn't do me much good with the world I lived in. Absently I ran my thumb along the silver and pearl bracelet I wore, courtesy of Martha Coiro. I thought back on the last day I had seen Davan, five years ago...

Davan laughed at his father's joke, catching my eye and smiling. I blushed a bit; he really was too handsome for words. He ruffled his golden blond hair with one hand, his blue eyes shining.

"Want to come for a walk?"

I jumped up eagerly.

"Yeah!" I grabbed his hand, looking at Mom for permission.

"Okay, you two go on ahead. Don't stay away too long."

Mom nodded and waved us on.

"Thanks, Mom."

Davan led the way as we left, my heart thrilling at the prospect of being alone with him.

"I love it out here. Don't you?"

"Yeah, it's beautiful."

I didn't notice Davan looking at me when he said that. The smell of fresh pine and lilacs was intoxicating, and I stopped to smell the flowers. He stepped closer as I straightened up.

"Um...I wanted...can I kiss you?"

I hesitated for a minute, then nodded. "Yeah. Yeah, okay."

He leaned down, carefully settling his mouth on mine. I felt uncomfortable and awkward with my head bent back, but I didn't want to stop. Just as his arm slipped around my waist, an angry shout broke us apart. I flushed all over when I saw Mom standing there. "Come back, you two. Now."

"Mrs. Ellis, we were just kissing –"

"There's no such thing as just a kiss, Davan."

Mom cut him off.

"You know about the Moral Laws?"

Davan lowered his eyes and nodded, his face turning red.

"Good. Then you understand why you can't do that again. Now come back, it's time to go."

My stomach knotted as I fell into step beside Mom. As I watched Davan walk ahead of me, I knew this would end badly...

I wiped my eyes, my stomach rumbling. I fished my sandwich out, taking an impatient bite and washing it down with a gulp of water. I swallowed the last piece and stood up, grabbing my knapsack. My lips tightened as I reminded myself not to lose the bracelet. I knew if that happened, I'd be in more trouble than I wanted to think about. The sounds of chatter and engines greeted me as I arrived at the bus stop, hoping I wouldn't have to wait too long for a ride home. I stopped short as I saw Martha Coiro sitting on the bench, flanked by her bodyguards. A petite, good-looking Hispanic woman who oversaw all relationships, she nonetheless struck fear into the hearts of the people. I backed up slowly, mentally cursing as her head turned in my direction.

"Miss Ellis, good morning."
She smiled at me, her dark brown bob framing her face.

"Uh...hi. Good morning, Ms. Coiro."
I gave a dutiful reply, feeling my legs start to shake slightly. Of the four Council members Martha, Lois Abbott, Gideon Hawke, and Yoshiro Bishop, I wasn't sure who I hated the most.

"Miss Ellis? I asked you a question."

I jumped.

"I beg your pardon, Ms. Coiro."

"That's quite all right. But it is bad manners, dear, to let your mind wander when having a conversation."

My face burned as I apologized.

"Yes ma'am. Excuse me, please. What was your question?"

"Are you prepared for July fourth?"

"As ready as I'll ever be...ma'am."

"And your...friend, Mr. Peters? He's in good health?"

"Yes, ma'am."

I felt my stomach clench when she mentioned Jerad, wondering if she questioned him about me. Thankfully, Martha stood to go, wishing me well as she boarded the trolley. I let my breath out in a whoosh of relief and sank onto the bench to wait for the next ride. The billboard across the street seemed to taunt me as it showed images of young people performing stunts and acrobatics, then navigating a treacherous maze, then finally an obstacle course. I was already seventeen, and I comforted myself with the fact that I hadn't been called even after three years of attending the choosing ceremony.

I jumped to my feet as the next trolley came to the curb, snagging a seat near the back. I scowled at the security camera in front; everywhere people were watched, presided over by the Council Four. *They just can't get enough, they must control everything, don't they?* The bitter thought trailed me as I disembarked at my street, tossing my long flaxen blonde hair over my shoulder. I stood in front of the mirror for a minute, staring at my dark brown eyes and round freckled face. I sighed; those freckles had always bothered me. I grabbed my reader and sprawled on my bed, soon losing myself in my favorite books. I didn't see Al sneaking in until he jumped on top of me. I shrieked and rolled over.

"Al!"

Al laughed and then yelped as he slipped off me and fell on the floor.

"You!"

I tickled him until he wriggled free and charged down the stairs.

"You're it! Come catch me!" He called.

I chased him into the backyard and tackled him again. He pelted me with a handful of leaves. I shook my hair out of my face and ducked as a stick went whizzing past me.

"Gabby?"

I grew serious and headed to the grotto at the edge of our property. Gabby stood by the fountain with Ethon, practicing her skills. She pushed her curly brown hair over one shoulder, her green eyes narrowed in concentration. She held out her hand as Ethon threw a rock, redirecting it towards the fountain. Ethon fired up his lighter, the flame growing until it encased his hand.

"Abagail?"

I raised my voice slightly, trying to ignore Ethon's angry look.

"You know you're not supposed to do that."

I stepped closer, motioning her away from the fountain.

"Oh, so that means I can't do this either?"

Gabby stepped into a small pile of dust, disappearing from the spot and reappearing a few seconds later at the edge of the garden. Ethon smiled proudly as a large rock thrown by Gabby bounced off him, his body wreathed in flames.

"Guys, stop it!"

"Hey, cool it."

Ethon pointed his finger at me, his brown eyes smoldering.

"We know what we're doing."

"What happens if one of us gets caught? Go ahead, guess."

"It's her gift, let her use it how she wants."

"Oh yeah, and let's start a war while we're at it."

"Maybe we should."

I froze; I couldn't believe he would be serious about that.

"Please tell me that's a joke."

Ethon glared at me.

"What do you think?"

"You two are crazy."

"And you're just too scared to do something. It's going to happen Dawnielle, and we damn well better be ready when it does!" Ethon shoved past me with Gabby on his heels. I blinked back tears as they headed back to the house. Al sidled up next to me.

"Ellie...could that happen? A war, I mean?"

"I don't know, Al." I ruffled his hair.

"Could we win?"

"Al, try not to think about that. You know, the circus is next month."

"What if they pick me?"

"Al, that's two years away. You're safe, I promise. Besides, I've been going for three years now, and I never got called." I grinned teasingly at him. "I won't let anything happen to you." I grew serious and wrapped an arm around his shoulders.

"Albern, Dawnielle! Lunchtime!"

Dad's voice was a welcome distraction from my frightening thoughts of next month. I felt better as Al put his arm around my waist. I helped myself to the spaghetti and garlic bread, snagging a seat next to Al, with Gabby on his other side.

"Dawnielle, are you ready for next month?"

Mom smiled at me, but I saw the worry in her eyes,

"Yeah, Mom. I'll be okay. I haven't been chosen yet, so I don't think this time will be any different."

Ethon raised his head from his plate.

"You should try for the Zodiac Circus."

I shrugged.

"I don't think I'll even get chosen; you know."

"Well, you should get ready even if –"

"Ethon, that's enough." Mom frowned at him.

I abruptly set my fork down and stood up.

"Can I be excused, please?

Dad nodded, his eyes on his plate. I left the table and grabbed my jacket and backpack before heading down the block to Jerad's house.

"Hello? Jerad?"

I knocked anxiously, peering through the curtain. The door cracked open, and Jerad emerged to give me a hug, his hazel eyes shining.

"Hey, Ellie. Come on in."

He led the way to his living room, where a checkers game board sat.

"You go first."

He sat across from me, smoothing his dark brown hair back. I moved the red checker forward. He laughed as he countered my next two moves.

"You always kick my butt when we play this

game."

"Well, chess is even better."

He grinned at me, toying with the top button on his shirt. A knock at the door jolted him to his feet. My heart sank as I saw an Inquirer for Martha Coiro standing in the doorway. Jerad remained calm as he answered the man's questions and explained that I was a visitor and close friend. The man frowned at me, but made no comments and left, leaving us in awkward silence.

"Want a soda?"

"Thanks. Your move."

Jerad jumped two red checkers and caught my eye.

"You know, Jerad...I think the only reason we haven't taken off is because of you guys."

Jerad nodded and escorted me to the door. I hugged him longer than intended, feeling a swell of affection deep inside that I didn't quite understand.

CHAPTER TWO

Two weeks later...

The sound of the birds woke me as I sat up, wincing at the prickling sensation in my hands. Al came bouncing in, dramatically flinging the curtains open and dousing the room in sunlight, turning his hair to pure gold.

"Breakfast time!"

He grinned at me, his brown eyes shining.

"Oh, yum. What are we having?"

"Waffles."

"My favorite."

I followed him downstairs and grabbed a seat between him and Anna.

"Morning."

Anna smiled at me with the same green eyes and brown hair Gabby had. But where Gabby was abrasive and rebellious, Anna was kind and patient.

"Morning."

"So, tomorrow's July fourth."

"Yeah. Maybe I'll get to be in the Zodiac Circus." I tried to smile but my stomach knotted at the thought. I bent my head and focused on my food, hoping to avoid any more questions. Ethon chatted with Gabby about which contest they would have liked best. I swallowed the last bite and stood up, dropping the dishes in the sink before heading into town. Up ahead several people were being branded with a letter D and displayed before a small crowd. My jaw clenched as I saw another group being loaded onto a truck for transport. I knew who they were: Deviants, those who refused to obey the laws. Ethon's words came back to me, and I sped up, wondering for a minute if he could be right about starting a war. I didn’t see Jerad coming down the street until I bumped into him, almost knocking him over.

"Oh God, I’m sorry. Hey."

"Hi, Ellie. Good to see you."

"Are you okay?" Jerad stared at me.

"Yeah...I saw things. You know..."

Jerad's eyes went stony for a second as he invited me for hot chocolate. I grabbed a table by the window as he came back with two mugs.

"Do you think the Council will ever be overthrown?"

"I don't know. Probably not for a long time."

"You know, I kind of feel like a coward sometimes."

"Hey." Jerad put a hand on my shoulder.

"You're not a coward. There's nothing anyone can do right now."

I nodded, my eyes on my cup.

"Ellie...Um, there's something that I need to tell you. I have to tell someone."

Jerad leaned in closer, putting his hand on top of mine. My heart skipped a beat.

"I do like you...but...there's things going on with me that I don't understand. I mean...I'm having feelings...towards boys."

He bit his lip, looking down. I knew what he meant and tried my best to comfort him.

"Jerad, it's okay."

I squeezed his hand, clumsily wrapping an arm

around his shoulders as he started to shake.

"It's okay, Jerad. I won't tell anyone."

He hugged me back, discreetly wiping his eyes.

"Thank you, Ellie."

I tried not to look at Jerad's bracelet as we left the cafe, cruising town until the sun began to set. I was sorely tempted to ask if I could stay the night with him, but I forced myself to say goodbye as we pulled up to my street.

"I'll see you tomorrow."

I waved as the trolley pulled away, walking to the door. I closed my eyes, trying to think about what I would do if Jerad got chosen. What if I got chosen? Three years, I reminded myself, three years I had gone and come back safely. And Anna had too, after being in the Gymnasium Circus. If she could do it, maybe I could too. I held on to that thought, indulging my imagination until I was called for dinner. I opened my eyes the next morning, glancing at the clock which read seven-thirty, July 4th. I pulled my clothes on before going outside to the garden, telekinetically playing around with sticks and leaves. A twig snapped and I sat upright, relieved to see it was

Gabby, who settled down next to me.

"Hey, morning. You ready for today?"

"Guess so."

"So, which one do you like best?"

"The Gymnasium one, I guess. But maybe I won't get chosen."

"You know, Ellie, you can't keep saying that. It actually looks like fun."

"Gabby, people die in these contests, they disappear, and you think it's a game. It's not fun."

"Well, I hope I get chosen. You will too, one day."

"Don't say that."

Gabby scoffed.

"I'm not afraid, Ellie."

I stood up.

"I'm not afraid either, but –"

"Yes, you are! You always say you won't get chosen, what if you do? You're just scared!"

"Well, maybe you should be too! It's just a way for them to bully us!"

"I'm not scared!"

Gabby teleported and landed a kick at my stomach. I sprawled on the ground, gasping. Anger surged through me, and I levitated a branch to hit her in the face.

"Hey!"

Dad was standing there, glaring at us.

"What's going on here?"

"Ellie hit me!"

"She thinks I'm a coward!"

I wiped my eyes.

"Gabby, is this true?"

"I didn't say that. She's just scared to be in the circus! It doesn't look that bad!"

"All right, enough! I don't care who started what; just go inside and cool off, both of you!"

I stalked back to the house, tears stinging my eyes.

"Ellie..."

"Gabby, go upstairs. I'll be up in a few minutes."

I stiffened as Dad motioned for me to sit at the bar.

"Want to tell me what happened?"

I started from when I'd seen Ethon and Gabby practicing their skills.

"It's been three years and I've never been chosen." I blew my nose. "And yeah, Dad, I am scared of that happening."

"I know, honey. It seems that you've been holding onto that hope. But if you do get picked, you should trust yourself, and you won't be alone in the arena."

I nodded. "I'll go apologize to Gabby –"

"No, honey." Dad smiled. "You can do that when you're ready."

I nodded and went to my room to pack a bag. I tried reading and tossed my book on the table, closing my eyes and listening to the birds, until Mom called me.

"Yeah, Mom."

"Okay, sweetie. Get your things and come downstairs, it's almost time to go."

CHAPTER THREE

I took a deep breath and grabbed my bag as we got out of the car. Mom put a hand on my shoulder as we arrived at the station. My voice sounded unnaturally steady as I said my goodbyes, hugging Al the longest. The boarding call was announced, and I stepped onto the train, waving before we disappeared around the corner. I stared out at the countryside; this was happening, for the fourth time in my life. I shook my head and snagged a compartment which held two narrow bunks and sank onto the bottom with a sigh. I looked up as a stocky Chinese girl came in.

"Oh, hi."

"Hey. Are you waiting for somebody?"

"No, it's all yours."

"Thanks." The girl extended her hand. "I'm Min."

"Dawnielle. Where are you from?"

"Laban."

"Me too." I smiled for the first time.

Min dumped her bag in the corner and clambered onto the top bunk, slipping a pair of earbuds on and humming. I shut my eyes, trying to take a nap. Sometime later, Min shook me awake.

"Hey, dinner time."

I sat up and rubbed my eyes, following her to the dining area. I wolfed down the macaroni and cheese I had been served, listening as Min told me that she'd had a brother who died in the Circus Labyrinthos.

"How old are you, Dawnielle?"

"Seventeen, same as you. Is this your first time?"

"Uh...no. This is my second time. I was in the Zodiac Circus. But we didn't win."

Min's jaw tightened. "One of my teammates got trampled."

"I'm really sorry. Um...my sister Anna was in the Gymnasium Circus. She said that's the best one."

"Which other town did they compete against?"

"Trellis."

"Lucky for her, I guess. But yeah, I always liked the Circus Gymnasium. But hell, I probably don't stand a chance."

"Maybe we will."

"Not against one of the twin cities." Min almost glared at me, and I fell silent. I couldn't think of anything else to say as we headed back to our compartment to bed. I squirmed for a few minutes to get comfortable and soon fell asleep.

Al reached out, his eyes imploring. I lunged forward, willing my gifts to work.

"Ellie..." The building collapsed, burying Al alive. I fell to my knees, tears streaming...

"No!"

The cry jolted me awake. I clutched the blanket, remembering that Al was at home with Mom and Dad. I shoved back the covers and hurried to dress before the train pulled into Abundantia city. Jerad waved enthusiastically as we got off. I stuck close to him as we made our way to the Morium's food court. Lois Abbott, head of the Council, stood by the doorway, glancing at me for a second before turning back to her bodyguards. I swallowed the lump in my throat and made sure to sit next to Jerad as we were served our meals. The smell of salmon alfredo was intoxicating, and I reached greedily for my fork. There was food everywhere it seemed, and I helped myself to more chocolate mousse. I had just swallowed the last bite when we were called to the Announcement Hall. I felt queasy as I was directed to sit with the girls, while Jerad went to the other side. The audience clapped politely as Lois took the podium, beginning her speech about the country's history:

> "Our country was once a thriving society. Everyone had what they needed, but when the earthquakes hit, the nation was torn apart. Chaos reigned and thousands died in the war for what resources remained. When the Council finally took over, peace and order was restored. And payment was, of course, expected. All of you here today, are doing your part to ensure the survival of the new nation."

There was another smattering of applause, and Lois began choosing the teams. Several groups came to the stage, and Lois called for Laban's team.

"Min Li Yang."

Min stepped forward; her head held high in defiance.

"Zane Johnson Carver." A tall Black boy came onto the stage, shaking from head to foot.

"Jerad Allen Peters."

I bit back a gasp as Jerad's arm shot up, signaling he was present.

"Dawnielle Marit Ellis."

Time stopped. There had to be a mistake. Three years, and my name hadn't been called once. Why would this time be any different?

"Dawnielle Marit Ellis."

At a nudge from the girl behind me, I took a step forward. I tripped on my long skirt and stumbled on the stairs, my face burning. Lois looked irritated as she extended her hand to me. I winced as she pulled me forward, directing me to stand beside Jerad. Jerad peeked over at me, offering a small smile in reassurance. Images flashed on the screen behind the stage as Lois assigned the teams to the Circuses:

"Circus Zodiac...Team Everest and Team Phineas. Circus Labyrinthos...Team Solaris and Team Sedge. Circus Gymnasium...Team Eve and Team Trellis. Circus Empodio...Team Phoebus and Team Laban."

My heart sank at the thought of going up against Phoebus...in the obstacle course. The picture of the Wood Traps didn't offer any comfort as we were ushered from the Announcement Hall and taken to a room in the Morium. I took a minute to breathe in the smell of fresh linen and paint as I sat down at the communication screen, dialing my family's residence. The picture came to life, and tears stung my eyes as I surveyed my home. The screen flashed a question:

Summon relative?

Abagail Ellis.

My hands shook as I typed Gabby's name. I tried to calm down as Gabby sat down, her eyes widening as she saw me.

"Ellie? Hi, how are you? Are you okay?"

"Yeah. I'm okay. I'm safe...for now."

"Which one was it?"

"Obstacle course. We're going up against Phoebus."

Gabby's face darkened, then to my surprise she wished me luck. "I know you'll do fine."

"What makes you say that?"

"Just a feeling."

"Uh...you know, I'm sorry about...earlier."

I squeezed my eyes shut; two tears spilled out. Gabby's lip quivered for a second, then her expression relaxed.

"Me too. Hey, you're going to come back, Ellie. I know you will."

She grinned at me with her familiar curling smile, and I touched the screen in a brief, silent farewell before heading to my room.

CHAPTER FOUR

I woke up at a sharp poke from Min, pulling my clothes on as she finished braiding her hair.

"What time is it?"

"Quarter to eight. Breakfast is at eight-thirty. Then we train."

The smell of fresh food settled my nerves as we sat down. I had just finished the pancakes before a bowl of fruit was placed in front of me. The server barely acknowledged my thanks and went to the next table. I ate as much as I could and gulped down the orange juice.

"Why do they feed us so much?" Min shrugged.

"The training, I guess. We need energy."

She swallowed the last bite on her plate and accepted another glass of milk. I surveyed Phoebus Team out of the corner of my eye. They were tall, strong, healthy-looking, and I could feel the confidence rolling off them in waves.

"Attention."

All noise stopped as Lois started roll call. The teams stood one by one as they were called and led away.

"Teams Laban, please proceed to Arena Conventus for training."

The Arena Conventus loomed ahead; I took a deep breath, staring around at the sections before spotting the obstacle course. One of the girls from Phoebus motioned me over.

"First time?" The girl smiled at me. Her jet-black hair and almond shaped eyes hinted at her Asian heritage.

I gave an ironic smile. "Yeah."

"How about a few rounds?"

"Um...okay."

"I'll go easy on you. I'm Kimiko, by the way. Call me Kimi." Kimi tossed her ponytail over her shoulder.

"Dawnielle."

Kimi bent in a runner's crouch. "Ready, and…go!"

She quickly overtook me as we navigated the ladders, ropes, and nets. I scrabbled for a hold on the chain-link net and tumbled off, cursing as I fell with a thump.

"Again." She motioned to me.

I stiffened but knew I had no choice. I cringed as my foot slipped but pushed myself forward. I shrieked as the ropes came from all sides, tangling relentlessly. I lashed out with my gift, the wooden frame buckling under my violent gestures. I wriggled loose, scrambling back onto the ladder.

"How the hell did you do that?" Kimi was gaping at me from the ground.

I glanced around and became acutely aware of everyone staring at me. "I'm...gifted."

“Like, telekinetic or something?” Kimi’s eyes widened.

“Something like that.” My face burned.

I noticed one of the guards whispering to his aide, who nodded and took off. I swallowed down my dread and turned back to the training area.

"Another round."

Kimi climbed up the ladder, waiting expectantly. I steeled myself for another painful bout, enduring several humiliating defeats before successfully navigating the nets. The other teams had stopped working, and I was relieved to see they were impressed. Jerad surveyed me with pride as training resumed. I opted to work alone, honing my stopping skills until the relief bell sounded. I winced as Min playfully threw an arm around my shoulders, the two of us laughing with the boys. For a precious few minutes, I forgot where we were as we shared funny stories. Two days later, I sat quietly practicing with my gift after breakfast until the knock on our door at noon. I glimpsed the forbidding Circus Empodio as we were led to the gate of Arena Facio. I shouldered the rucksack given to me by the guard and stepped through the gate, gaping at the stone valley ahead. The weight of my rucksack didn't make me feel much better, but I reminded myself that I had Jerad. I stared at the screen as it counted the last ten seconds. A horn sounded, and I lunged forward, sprinting after Min. The obstacles seemed to come from everywhere: stone walls rose and fell, the ground opened and closed at will. I shrieked as the ground disappeared beneath my feet, the rough stone scraped my face as I clawed at the ground. Jerad was there, grabbing frantically for my arm.

"Reach! Come on!"

"God! Jerad, I can't!"

My fingers slipped and to my horror, I lost my grip. I thrashed and kicked as I fell, telekinetically calling up a pair of rocks to boost myself back to the surface. The ground closed, burying me in darkness. I pounded the ceiling, to no avail. I clenched my teeth as I realized that Lois must have ordered extra precautions on account of my gifts. I retreated to the ground and stared at the trio of tunnels before deciding to go straight ahead.

CHAPTER FIVE

Electricity crackled in my fingers and lit the way as I rounded the corner, swallowing hard at the sight of human bones. The sound of gurgling made me speed up, growing louder until I almost stepped right into the bubbling stream. For a few seconds I refused to believe my eyes, then I threw myself down by the edge and drank, filling my bottle to the brim. I took a moment to rest, wondering how long it would take for me to reach the surface. I jumped at a loud thump up ahead and picked up a large rock. I began to back out of sight slowly when Kimi stumbled out of the shadows, clutching her ankle.

"Kimi? What happened?"

Kimi chuckled. "That's what you get for being cocky." She tried to stand and grunted in pain. "Damn it...I think it's definitely sprained."

"I have an idea. Let me help you."

I took her arm and hoisted her on her feet, helping

her to the stream.

"What are you doing?"

Kimi stared at me with a quizzical expression. I didn't answer, but set her injured foot in the stream, concentrating. My hands warmed, glowing electric blue. Kimi pulled her leg out of my grasp, and as I had hoped, she was able to stand.

"Okay, what did you do to me?"

"I can heal through water."

"So, you have the power of nature, and you can also heal...with water?"

I nodded. "Actually, it's the power of the industrial elements. Metal, stone, wood, electricity."

Kimi laughed, trying to take it in. I braced myself when the floor began to rise and felt a rush of relief when sunlight seared my eyes. Kimi set off, motioning for me to follow her.

"What happens when we finish?"

"Whoever wins, gets to go on like usual."

"Um, what happens to the losers?"

Kimi's expression grew sour. "You win, or you die trying."

We trudged ahead grimly, neither of us saying

anything else. Kimi tensed when she heard people talking up ahead.

"That's my team."

I recognized Jerad's voice and turned to Kimi. Wordlessly, I shook hands with her; watching as she ducked back into the shadows. I didn't notice Zane's jealous look as Jerad hugged me in relief. I sat down gratefully, taking a minute to eat and drink. I watched with apprehension as the sky grew darker. I tried using my pack as a pillow and watched the stars come out until I drifted off.

"Hey, Ellie. Wake up."

Jerad shook me awake and helped me to my feet. I shouldered my pack and set off after the others. I dodged another obstacle and slid down the final stairway as it went flat. For a second, I was caught up in the rush, and then glimpsed the end up ahead. I pushed myself faster, not stopping until I reached the exit. I laughed to myself as my teammates appeared behind me.

Lois's voice boomed over the public address system.

"Congratulations, Laban. Proceed to the Wood Traps."

Her voice seemed to remind me that this was not for fun.

"Where's the other team?"

The question came out before I could stop myself.

Zane glared at me. "They're not our concern."

"I just want to know if they're okay."

"They're way ahead of us. That's all we need to know."

Zane set off without a backward glance, the rest of us following suit. The snap of a branch alerted me to the trap overhead. I dove forward, sprawling on my belly and spitting out a mouthful of leaves. I rolled away as another trap opened underneath me. I spotted Min up ahead and barreled toward her, not seeing the trap until it closed around me. I felt a thrill of dread as I was hoisted into the air, suspended twenty feet above the forest floor. I gritted my teeth and shoved, cheering inside when the bars broke apart in my hands. I stopped when I heard a sickening crack, followed by a scream. In horror I saw a member of Phoebus Team falling. My arm shot out to make two branches catch him. He stared at me in shock as I lowered him to the ground.

"Thanks a lot!" He turned towards me and gave a grateful salute.

"Yeah. Hey! What's your name?"

"Mordecai!"

He called back before going after his group. I glimpsed my team going ahead and forced myself to calm down. Drawing a deep breath, I reached out, the branches arranging themselves as a stairway. I steeled myself and jumped from one limb to the next. My foot slipped and I fell down the last ten feet, landing hard on my wrist. I rolled painfully onto my knees and leaned against a nearby tree. Blood trickled down from a gash on my forehead. Cradling my injured arm, I started forward. I kept counting the numbers in my head as I pushed myself on, grinning when I saw the lake. I collapsed in the shallow waters and passed out as my injuries healed themselves; not hearing my team come back for me.

CHAPTER SIX

I came to, warmed by the fire, a spare jacket draped over my back. Zane offered me a box of crackers and water, eyeing me with concern and a hint of anger. I stared back, asking if he had something to say.

"Why did you help that boy?"

"Why not?"

"He's not a member of our team."

"I'm not letting him die just because –"

Zane slammed his fist against the ground and leaned in closer.

"You can't do that! It's against the rules! And you're going to get hurt!"

"I don't care –"

"Well, you should!"

"Why?" I finally stood up.

"Because they'll come after your family! They take someone you love and throw them in the arena and make it twice as hard! And they will die because of you!"

"Stop it!"

Jerad shoved him back, Min jumping between them.

"Hey, cut it out!"

She glared at the boys. Zane grudgingly apologized as he passed by me, Jerad glowering after him. My hands shook as I followed the others. I had been sure helping Kimi and her teammate was the right thing to do, but now I just felt sick about it. I forced myself back to the present and dodged another trap, jumping away as it shot out of the ground like a shark, snapping shut inches from my ankles. I took a running leap over the next underground device, Jerad and the others right on my heels as the traps came from all directions.

"Heads up!"

Zane pointed upward; the team scattered. I scuttled away on all fours, narrowly avoiding another cage. Swatting a branch out of my face, I darted around the next contraption, almost tripping in my haste. Zane called a five-minute rest when the exit came into view, sitting next to Jerad. I caught the surreptitious look between them and wondered what was up before we were off again. I struggled to keep pace with Min as we came to the end of the course; my lungs burned and my legs felt like rubber, but I straightened immediately when I heard Lois's voice again.

> "Admirable performance, Laban Team. Continue please, to the Steel Forest. May your luck and your...heroics see you through to the end."

I stiffened a bit, getting the distinct impression that she was talking to me. I ignored Zane's pointed look and set my jaw as I stared ahead at the ominous maze of metal. Tentatively I stepped forward, then broke into a run, just missing a stab in the waist. Jerad yelped as he dodged another serrated blade aiming for his arm. I took a deep breath and stopped thinking, weaving through the course. I cringed at a sharp pain in my arm, then another in my leg. Hopping and jumping, I was forced to zigzag, ducking at one turn and diving to the ground at the next. A shriek ripped through the arena as one member of Phoebus Team was maimed and then stabbed through the side. I gagged at the sight and stumbled away, keeping my eyes on Zane's back. At another scream from the other side, something in me snapped. Waving my arms while running, I forced the blades back, catching sight of Kimi leading her remaining teammates through the maze. Red filled my vision and I tasted blood as Jerad seized my arm, pulling me out of reach of the next spike. Zane and Min were neck and neck, he jumped over the next obstacle as she went under it. I stumbled and collapsed on my knees, panting from sheer exhaustion. Jerad skidded to a halt, rushing back and pulling me on my feet.

"I can't..." I swallowed painfully, unable to say anything more.

"It's almost over. Come on." Jerad threw my arm around his shoulders. "We're going to make it, Ellie."

The two of us sprinted the last fifty yards; we crossed the finish line with Team Phoebus almost right next to us, all of us drenched in sweat and bleeding.

CHAPTER SEVEN

"Congratulations, teams. This is a day of days." Lois addressed the arena; I imagined her gloating pleasure and clenched my teeth, waiting for the axe to fall.

"I declare Team Laban...winners of the Circus Empodio."

Min erupted with a scream of ecstasy, Zane and Jerad high-fived one another and embraced before Lois continued. "Team Phoebus shall retrain...for the Circus Gymnasium."

Kimi sagged, cradling her head in her hands. Mordecai patted her shoulder awkwardly, eyeing us with envy. Their other teammate, a teenaged Polynesian girl, looked away with a hard expression. Mordecai froze when several medics came out with a stretcher carrying a young boy's body. One of them came up to me with a roll of gauze and tape.

"You're bleeding."

I felt something sticky on my cheek and cringed as I wiped my forehead too quickly, realizing my left eye was hurt. The young woman patched me up and left without another word.

"Winston."

I jumped, finding Mordecai standing next to me. He gawked at the patch for a second.

"His name was Winston."

"I'm sorry."

"Yeah." He drew a sharp breath. "What are you going to do now?"

"Go home, I guess."

I clapped him on the shoulder, following my team out of the arena and back to the Morium. We stood next to the other victorious teams Eve, Solaris, and Phineas as each was commended for their performance. I saw the vacant look in a Solaris member's eyes and could only imagine what she had seen before Lois mentioned Laban.

"Laban, for your efforts, you are awarded."

A male assistant approached us with four medals. I held myself rigid as he placed mine over my neck.

After the celebratory dinner, I collapsed in my bed, telling myself over and over that I was done. I woke up the next morning and ducked into the bathroom, slowly peeling off the eyepatch. Running a wet washcloth over my face, I sighed with relief as my face returned to normal. I came out to find Min sitting out on the balcony.

"Morning." She indicated a seat next to her.

I accepted the cup of tea she handed me. "Are you okay?"

"Yeah." Min rubbed her eyes. "We won. What are the odds?"

I couldn't think of anything to say and just nodded.

"So, you and Jerad...is there something there?"

I knew what she meant and quickly clarified.

"Well, sometimes I feel like it. But he's more like the brother I never had. And anyway, there's somebody else that I met a while back. But he's not around anymore."

My jaw quivered as my eyes started to well up. Min patted my arm reassuringly.

"It's okay. Not sure if I'd want a boyfriend. Especially now with Miss Martha and all her rules."

Her mouth twisted bitterly at the mention of Martha's name. I forced thoughts of the Council out of my head, although I silently resolved to talk to Davan after we returned home. Later, I sat at the communications desk, searching for Davan's address. I sent him a note telling him I was safe and to contact me tomorrow. I swallowed hard as I got up to pack my things, praying for my plan to go smoothly. While everyone slept on the train, I lay awake until around midnight, too exhausted to think anymore.

"Ellie. Hey, wake up." Jerad shook my shoulder insistently. "We're almost home."

"Oh."

I sat up, not caring that my bare legs were visible as I excused myself to get dressed.

My heart leaped when I saw several families standing at the platform. Mom and Dad both came forward to hug me, Ethon smiled as I turned to him.

"You won."

He tousled my hair.

"You know, Gabby said you would."

He gazed at me seriously. My vision blurred as he

wrapped an arm around my shoulders, Al trying to embrace both of us at once. Gabby clambered into the backseat next to me.

"I knew you were going to make it." She whispered to me. I drew a shaky breath and nodded thanks.

"I'm glad you don't have to go back."

"So am I."

For the first time in years, I could feel a connection with her. I slipped an arm around her shoulders as we arrived home. The home screen flashed a message addressed to me. I swallowed hard as I was left to answer it privately. Davan's face lit up the screen.

"Hey there, champion."

I smiled. "Hi Davan."

"You said you wanted to talk."

"Yeah. I want...I want to go public." I looked straight at him. "With you."

Davan sighed uneasily. "You sure about that? You know what that means."

"I don't care. I'm...Davan, I'm ready. I want this. Do you love me?"

"Yes." Davan swallowed hard. "I love you,

Dawnielle." He nodded firmly. "Okay, let's do this."

My throat tightened as I said good night, touching my index finger to the screen. The next morning, I opened my eyes to Gabby calling me to breakfast, reluctantly pulling my clothes on. The smell of eggs and butter greeted me as I entered the kitchen. I sat next to Al, trying not to toy with my food too much as Mom and Dad discussed their next big project. As Dad headed out the door, I quickly excused myself and caught up to him as he was about to get in the car.

CHAPTER EIGHT

"Dad! Dad, wait! I need to tell you something. I talked with Davan yesterday. And we've decided to announce we're a couple." I braced myself for a lecture as Dad paused.

"Are you sure you want to do that?"

"Yeah. I'm sure. Um...you're not going to tell me that's a bad idea?"

"I don't want to see you hurt. You know what happens to people who break the rules."

"I know, Dad. That's not going to happen."

"You're going to have to get engaged. You won't have any peace anymore, and you're only seventeen. This is the rest of your life –"

"Dad, please. Trust me, I know what this means. But I'm ready."

Dad sighed and ground his jaw for a second, then his expression softened.

"Okay, honey." He hugged me before driving away.

I watched his car until it turned the corner. Mom seized my arm as I came inside and ordered me to go to the living room.

"Councilwoman Coiro wants to talk to you. Dawnielle, what's going on? Tell me quickly."

"Davan and I want to be connected. I mean, that we want to go public. I talked to him yesterday. And I know what I'm doing, Mom."

"Dawnielle –"

"If I can win in the Circus, I can do this. I can do it, Mom. Please."

My eyes stung as I looked at her.

"I just...I can't do this if you don't support me. You said you trusted me."

I turned away, waiting for her refusal, and was shocked when she put her arm around me.

"It's them I don't trust. The Council, their soldiers. When I went public, it wasn't with Harvey. I was barely older than you, nineteen. And I broke off my engagement when I fell in love with your father. And this is what I got for it."

She showed me an ugly brand in the shape of a D on her upper arm.

"I didn't wait for permission to be with your father. That's how it works. The last thing I want is for that to happen to you."

I gaped at the mark, on the verge of changing my mind when I thought of that day in the Grove five years ago, and the Circus. I became calm and still, knowing what I wanted.

"That's not going to happen, Mom. I promise."

Mom gave a reluctant nod of acceptance.

"All right."

I turned to the flashing home screen and spoke Martha's name. My hands curled into fists as I stared at her image.

"Can you hear me, Dawnielle dear?"

"Yes."

"Am I correct in hearing this information: you and Davan Hier of Everest town wish to publicly connect yourselves?"

"Yes, ma'am. That's right."

"Very well. I shall expect the two of you in Abundantia, and come to Troy, in a week's time.

Best of luck to both of you."

Her abrupt tone stung, but I forced out a polite goodbye and slowly unclenched my fists as the screen shut off. Mom's arm tightened around me, and I leaned against her, crying myself out. I swallowed hard and punched in Davan's number, ducking my head as tears welled up again.

"Hey Davan, it's me again."

"What's up?"

"Martha said yes. So, it looks like we're going to Troy. One week, she said."

"Okay. Are you going to be all right?"

I drew a deep breath, wiping my eyes and trying to stand up straight.

"Yeah, I'll be okay. I'll see you soon."

"Ok. See you in a week."

We shared a smile at that. I turned to Mom, who was sorting several figurines on the table, but I could tell she'd heard everything.

"Can I go to the Grove? Just...just by myself."

"All right. But be back before dinner. No excuses, Dawnielle."

"Yes, Mom." I gave her a quick hug before

grabbing my knapsack by the door. I fidgeted during the ride, twisting the shoulder straps in my hands before my stop came up.

The Grove was quiet as ever; I dumped my bag on the ground before taking a running start. A tree root rose from the ground as I stepped on it, launching myself into the air. The trees danced around me as I jumped from branch to branch, and I threw caution to the wind until I wore myself out. I spun around when I saw someone out of the corner of my eye. Min started to back up, but I motioned her over.

"What's up?"

"Nothing, really."

She plopped down beside me. "That was awesome, what you did."

"Thanks. But...please don't tell anybody."

"No, of course not."

"Well, Lois already knows, but I guess it doesn't matter whether I use it or not."

"She's not going to hurt you. She's got no proof you did anything, and anyways, we're like heroes now."

"It's not just me I'm worried about. Gabby and Ethon have gifts too. Like me, I mean."

Min's eyes widened. "Really?"

"Yeah, but...people don't know about that, and I want to keep it that way."

"Yes, ma'am." Min gave a sarcastic salute.

"So, really, what's going on?"

"I've decided...I'm going to Canada. My dad's cousin is there. I just can't, I can't live like this anymore." Min lowered her eyes, her jaw tightening.

I could see she really meant it. "When are you planning on going?"

"End of this year."

"Wish you luck. Hey, can I show you something cool?"

"Sure."

She followed me through the brush as I led her to an old library building.

"Behold!" I coughed at the taste of dust as the door swung open. "All the books you could want."

"I thought they got rid of these."

"Lucky us."

I pulled a couple books from a nearby shelf and almost dropped them when a brown-haired stranger appeared in the doorway. The man watched us with cool gray eyes, one arm resting against the doorjamb.

"Um...hi. What's your name?"

"Randolph Earl. You can call me Wolf. And who are you two?"

Min gave a slight wave as she introduced herself. "I'm Min. Nice to meet you."

"Dawnielle." I set the books down as he extended his hand to me.

"Both of you follow me, please."

Randolph made a curt gesture, clearly expecting us to obey him. Min exchanged a worried frown with me before reluctantly following the man. He led us deeper into the Grove, where I was surprised to find a neat dirt path had been recently made. I hesitated before stepping inside after Min, as Randolph spoke with a young girl acting as a guard.

"Tell Siren I have two witnesses."

"Wait. What does that mean, witnesses? We didn't see anything. Who the hell is Siren?" My voice rose at the last word.

Randolph turned to face me, and I saw for the first time how serious the situation was.

"Siren and I are the leaders of the Seventh Ring, and we have all taken a vow of resistance. If any of us should find you here again, you will be asked to join."

"Why? What if we don't want to?"

"Because that won't be an option for much longer. War is about to be declared. But not by us. The Council doesn't want the public to know or believe it. And we will save as many as we can."

"Who's declaring it?" I asked.

"Lois Abbott and Yoshiro Bishop. The last ten years, we've been nearly torn apart because manpower is scarce and resources even more so. But now there is a chance to take down the Council for good, and we can't afford to wait anymore. That was our first mistake, waiting for the right time. But there really isn't a 'right time'. So, if I invite you through this door, you are sworn to silence. Understood?"

"Yes, sir."

I stood up as straight as I could, almost giving a

salute.

An African-American woman with close cropped hair and feathered earrings glanced up as we entered, introducing herself as Elaine Rafferty. Min and I shook hands with her, and I knew this must be the woman called Siren.

"Elaine, this is Dawnielle, and Min." Randolph pointed to each of us in turn.

"Welcome to our humble hideout."

She smiled briefly before handing us a pair of necklaces.

"These are for you. You'll keep it with you at all times, until you decide to become members, after which you'll wear the rings."

"Wait a minute. You say that like we have no choice."

Min pulled me aside. "Dawnielle, I don't think there is a choice anymore."

"Didn't you want to leave?"

"Hey," Min's eyes bored into mine. "I'm going to make that decision, not you. I just...maybe there is another solution than just packing up and hitting the road."

I gathered my courage as I turned to speak with Elaine.

"I don't want to be a member right now. I mean, I can't. There's something I need to do."

I prayed she wouldn't ask further and was relieved when she nodded.

"I understand. You don't have to explain. But keep the necklace."

I stiffened slightly, realizing that it wasn't a request. We said a polite goodbye and were escorted out, taken to the edge of the Grove. I started to jog slowly when I saw the trolley come around the corner. "Want to ride with me?"

"Sure."

Min followed me as I boarded. "My house is before yours, I think."

We were silent on the way home; I leaned my head back against the seat while Min glanced out her window, fiddling with her necklace. I badly wanted to know what she had decided to do, but a voice in my head warned me it wasn't a good idea to pressure her. She reached for the bell to signal the driver. I stood to let her out and awkwardly gave her a hug goodbye.

"I'll see you around, yeah?" She flashed a brief grin.

"Uh...sure. Take care." I swallowed hard, taking my seat again.

As my street came up, I shoved the necklace in my knapsack, feeling an immense relief as I went through the front door. Gabby called for me from the dining room. She looked up from setting the table.

"Hey. Not late, am I?"

"No." She chuckled. "You and the Grove and the books."

"Well, it's an escape, isn't it?"

"Yeah. A distraction, Mom would call it."

"Yeah. I'm going to go change. I'll be right back."

I hurried to my room, pulling on a fresh pair of slacks and a sweater. I heard the door slam and went to greet Mom.

"Mom. Hi, Dad."

Dad smiled. "Hi, sweetie. Did you have a nice walk?"

"Yeah. I uh...I ran into one of the competitors, Min. From my team."

"That's nice."

Gabby sat next to me with Anna on my other side,

the smell of fresh garlic bread making my mouth water. I couldn't help but wonder what Davan was up to right now, maybe doing the exact same thing, eating dinner with his family. I shut my eyes for a second, forcing those thoughts out of my head. The cook placed a dish of apple crisp in front of me before slipping back to the kitchen. After dessert, Anna caught up with me at the stairs.

"I heard you and Davan are getting engaged."

"Yeah. And please, before you say that's a bad idea, I have thought about this –"

"No. God, Dawnielle, I was only eighteen myself, so I'm the last person to tell you that. I'm just worried, I know Mom told you what happened to her. I was engaged once; it was right after I got chosen for the Circus. It didn't work out. And I haven't tried since."

Anna looked away, her jaw stiffening.

"I remember that. I'm sorry. What was his name again?"

"Warner. Warner Roswell. He's...He's in Troy now, working for Yoshiro Bishop." Her lips tightened.

"Is that why you broke up with him?"

"I didn't. He left me. I refused to support the system, or his decision to work for Bishop, so he left me in the dust."

I almost said something sarcastic, but seeing the look on Anna's face, I decided to let the chips fall where they would in my case and thanked her.

"Thanks, Anna. But you don't have to worry. If that does happen, then I'll know."

I shut my bedroom door, twisting the necklace under my shirt.

CHAPTER NINE

I set my suitcase on the floor and stared in the mirror one last time. The blue silk sundress felt like heaven as I touched the looped French braid at the back of my head. I stumbled a bit in my wedge sandals as I came down the stairs, gripping the rail for support. Dad beamed proudly at me, and I couldn't resist twirling on the way out to the car. As we rounded the last corner, my heart began to pound. I forced myself to remain calm as Mom and Dad helped me with my luggage. Al handed me a keychain with a faded gray rabbit's foot.

"This'll be lucky for you." He smiled up at me.

"Thanks, Al."

Gabby gently urged him out of the way. "I'll see you." She swallowed hard and carefully embraced me. I stifled a laugh at her sudden cautiousness. I almost jumped onto the train, thoughts of what lay ahead making it impossible to sit still. The scenery slowly changed from trees to buildings as we entered Troy. I gaped at the shining gold structures, almost forgetting why I was here. A voice calling my name jerked my attention back to the present as a brunette wearing a beige skirt and blouse came up to me. I remembered that she was one of Martha's when I saw the color.

"Are you Dawnielle Marit Ellis?"

"Yes."

I gripped the rabbit's foot in my pocket as she curtly motioned for me to follow her, explaining that she worked for Martha. Curious though I was about other uniforms The Council's personnel wore, I kept silent as we drove through town. My heart soared as I spotted Davan sitting outside. I hugged him, forcing myself to be chaste as he offered me his arm. The smell of fresh paint and varnished wood permeated the hall as we were escorted to Martha's office. The room was large and heavily decorated with roses and paintings, the walls painted scarlet. Martha entered, greeting us in her usual cool, polite manner. The female aide quickly curtsied and stepped aside, standing against the wall.

"Follow me, please." Martha led us into a brightly lit adjoining room, where we stood side by side.

"Put these on."

Davan gave me a questioning look as he slipped one of the gold pendants over my neck, then his own.

"Now, you will take your vows. Repeat after me. I, Davan Lange Hier –"

"*I, Davan Lange Hier –*"

"Pledge myself to be bound, by law and in spirit."

"*Pledge myself to be bound, by law and in spirit.*"

"To Dawnielle Marit Ellis, from this day forward, until natural circumstances shall separate us."

"*To Dawnielle Marit Ellis, from this day forward, until natural circumstances shall separate us.*"

"And now..." Martha looked at me expectantly.

I said the declaration as calmly as I could, certain I would break down at any second.

"*I, Dawnielle Marit Ellis, pledge myself to be bound, by law and in spirit, to Davan Lange Hier, from this day forward, until natural circumstances shall separate us.*"

I hastily wiped my eyes before tears fell and exchanged rings with Davan, slipping the gold band over his finger.

Martha smiled; for the first time her emotion seemed genuine.

"You are now bonded with each other. Let the rings remind you always of the vow you have both taken."

The pearl's sheen made me feel slightly better as we were escorted to our new apartment on the third floor. I tried not to be too taken with the impressive decor, but despite myself I breathed in the fresh paint and surveyed the view outside with pleasure. Davan carefully slipped an arm around my shoulders.

"Well, Mrs. Hier...what shall we do now?"

"I don't know. Are you hungry? Because I am."

My stomach started to rumble as we headed into town. A swinging sign emblazoned with flowers caught my attention.

"Hey, let's try there."

"Okay."

Davan led the way inside, asking for a table for two. A server in her twenties came promptly, handing us our menus.

"Welcome to Marigold's Garden. I'm Marsha, I'll be your server this afternoon. We have been voted the Most Popular Restaurant three years in a row. Our special today is beef stroganoff, which is a particular favorite."

"I'll try that."

Davan grinned at Marsha, who beamed. I tried to keep the jealous edge out of my voice as I ordered the tuna casserole.

"That's another great dish."

"Thanks."

I handed back my menu. "She seems very nice."

Davan's jaw shifted as he readily agreed. "Yeah, but she's not you, Dawnielle."

"Well, um...did you ever get with anyone else since...since you left?"

Davan's eyes clouded a bit, as if I'd reminded him of something painful. "Yeah, I have. There were...several other girls."

I felt a sharp twinge of envy at hearing that, but Davan was quick to reassure me.

"But they were not you." He chuckled. "I'm engaged now."

We shared a laugh at that, our food arriving rather quickly.

"Did you know Gabby's a teleporter?"

"Seriously?"

"Yeah, and my brother Ethon, um...he can control plasma, like fire and stuff."

"And all this time, you guys never told anyone?"

"God, how could we?"

I fought back a quiver of dread. "The way things are now; they'd come for us armed to the teeth."

Davan looked down and stabbed a piece of food with his fork. We finished the rest of the meal in silence; I toyed with my chocolate trifle until the check came. Davan took it, insisting that he could pay. I couldn't resist taking a deep breath as we stepped outside. Davan stopped, leaning forward. I stood up on tiptoe, letting him slide his arm around my waist as he kissed me. I pulled away when I noticed an Inquirer staring at us with clear disapproval.

Davan took a pointed step back and asked if I wanted to stay out longer.

"No, let's just go back."

I turned my back on the man watching us and gripped Davan's hand tightly as we headed to the trolley stop. The apartment smelled of flowers and fresh linen as we arrived back at our new home. Davan slid his arm around my shoulders as we sat and watched the sunset until a guard cleared his throat insistently.

"Let's go, son."

Davan frowned. "I can't stay with her?"

"Not until you're married. You sleep separately until then."

Anger flared in Davan's eyes. "Hey, just who do you think you are?"

"I advise you do what you're asked, son."

The guard patted the baton on his hip, making his intentions clear.

Slowly, Davan stood up, his jaw clenched as he gave me a quick hug good night.

"See you in the morning."

"Good night, Davan."

Grudgingly, Davan followed the man out of my room. The ring did little to comfort me as I climbed into bed, dreading the next day.

I jolted awake the next morning at a chiming noise across the room, stumbling over to activate the screen.

Min's face appeared, her expression turning contrite.

"Oh, morning. Sorry I woke you up."

"Yeah, don't worry about it." I yawned. "What's up?"

"I just wanted to let you know...I've decided to join the Seventh Ring."

I stopped in mid-stretch and absorbed the news.

"Are...are you sure that's what you want?"

"Oh yeah. I'm positive."

She saw the look on my face and asserted that she knew what she was doing.

"Listen, you don't have to worry about me. I promise, I know what I'm doing."

"Okay. Just...you be careful."

"Yes, Mom." Min chuckled a bit. "This is it, man. War...it's coming. And I know that's not what you want. But I wanted to let you know, they'll take whoever they can get."

"Well, when has what we wanted ever mattered?"

I could almost taste my bitter tone. Min knew what I was talking about and glanced down for a second before saying good-bye. I swallowed hard, wondering who else would take a side before I would have to myself. I jumped when the door opened, Davan stopped short when he saw the stricken look on my face.

"What is it?"

"Davan, I have to tell you something. You're going to want to sit down."

His eyebrows rose as he sat on the bed next to me.

"You know, Min, my teammate... she's joined the Seventh Ring."

Davan went still. "I thought all that stuff was just rumors."

"No, it's real. I met them, me and Min, I mean. We met them before I came here. Please, don't tell anyone. This has to stay between us."

"Hey." Davan put a finger to my lips. "I'm not going to tell anybody. I promise."

I hugged him, the two of us sprawling across the bed. Neither of us saw the tiny camera recording us in the room as we got more involved.

CHAPTER TEN

The door flew open, two Inquirers marching in and pulling us on our feet.

"Hey, what is this?" Davan yelped in shock when the man twisted his arm behind his back.

"Stop it!" I shouted. "Leave him alone!"

A burst of light shot from my hand, hitting the Inquirer holding Davan. Suddenly my legs turned to jelly, I sank on the floor twitching uncontrollably. My captor stood over me, clutching a baton armed with a shocking device. Davan gave a roar of rage and lunged at the man, who round kicked him in the head, knocking him to the floor.

The two men carried us to Martha's office. My head swam as she charged us with flouting the boundaries of affection and ordered us separated, sentencing us to two years apart.

"And Dawnielle...I've been told to show you this,

by order of Lois Abbot."

Martha activated a screen on the wall, revealing the obstacle course's Wood Traps. I saw myself helping the boy called Mordecai, lowering him to safety.

Martha shook her head. "You understand...rules are rules. And you broke them."

Before I could speak, she shut the screen off and ordered us out. I feebly reached for Davan's hand before the agent pulled me away, taking me to a separate room. I lay on the bed, tears running into the pillows and watching as the sky grew darker, wondering if Mom had been right after all.

Two years later...

I rolled over at the sound of the bolt being slid back; a woman stood there with a tray of food. I took it without a word, eating as slowly as possible while she waited. She gave me a dirty look as she disappeared and came back with a modest beige dress and matching sandals.

"Martha wants to see you both."

My heart jumped at hearing about Davan. "Where's

Davan? Is he okay?"

The woman gave a noncommittal shrug. "Should be."

I bit back my scathing thoughts and got dressed, not wanting to think about what Martha may have decided.

My stomach lurched as the man who arrested me came into the room, attaching a large bracelet to my wrist.

"What –"

"Martha's orders. It's a Restraint."

I remembered the baton and took the hint. The guard led the way to Martha's quarters. Davan was physically restrained from embracing me as I entered and was seated in the chair three feet away. Martha observed both of us coldly as she informed us that our punishment was lenient considering we were both first time offenders. I wished I could murder her with my eyes as she pardoned us but maintained we would now be surveilled for our own safety. My hatred grew as the Inquirers took us back to our old apartment. After several hours of pacing in the other room, I asked to go outside.

"Very well." My Inquirer led the way downstairs.

I blinked at the bright sun, but the city's luxury no longer impressed me. My lips tightened as I reminded myself what I now knew. The billboard across the street began showing the Circus, and I realized it must be close to July.

"What's the date today?"

"July 3rd, Miss."

Al. Gabby. I remembered they were now fourteen years old. When the Maze came up, I was horrorstruck at the images of increased obstacles.

"They have to get through that?"

The man was unfazed by my shrill tone. "The contest changes every now and again. Makes it more exciting."

I mentally cursed Lois's name and Martha's as I was taken back. I gathered my courage and halted by Martha's door.

"May I speak to Martha, please?"

"Of course."

Martha looked up, smiling as though greeting an old friend. I resisted the urge to spit at her as I took a seat.

"I wanted to ask a favor. If you would give me

permission."

"For what, my dear?"

"I'd like to witness the next Contest Choosing. My...my brother and sister are both now of age, and it's tomorrow."

"They're both fourteen, now, you say?"

"Yes, ma'am." I forced the last word out.

"Then they're twins?"

"Yes, ma'am. I would like to be there, since it's their first time."

"Very well. But I will expect you back promptly afterwards." She gave me a stern look.

I stood up, saying a reluctant thank-you. The next day, I rose at seven am sharp and hurried to shower and dress, sharing a tense breakfast with Davan while two guards watched us. I rubbed my thumb over the bracelet I wore, knowing there was no way I could take it off. Hours passed, until Martha contacted me that it was time to go. As the train pulled into Olympia, I shrieked with joy at seeing Al's familiar posture. He and Gabby tackled me, all of us trying to pretend we weren't crying.

"Hey, what's that on your wrist?"

"Tracking device, I guess. I got in a little trouble with Martha. But I'm okay, I promise."

I examined Al. "I swear, you've grown a foot since I last saw you."

Al grinned briefly. "Two years."

I remembered my detainment and went somber. "Davan and I were under house arrest. We...we got caught in bed together."

"You mean...?" Al's eyebrows rose.

"No, we didn't actually...do anything. But we were separated for two years for it."

I glanced up at the warning bell tolling.

Gabby grabbed my hand. "We have to go, guys."

We hurried to catch up to the rest of the group at the Morium. I shut my eyes at the old memories of the place, when the public address system called my name. I went cold inside at recognizing Lois's voice. I got up and dutifully walked to where she was seated at the doorway with two guards.

"Hello, Dawnielle."

"Hi."

"I just received word from Martha Coiro that you wished to be here." Lois seemed oddly happy.

"Yes. It's...my brother and sister, it's their first time coming."

"All right. Since you have her permission."

Lois curtly signaled one of her guards, who escorted me back to the table where Al and Gabby sat. Lois summoned everyone to the Announcement Hall as lunch ended. I was sad to see Al and Gabby forced to sit in the first row, while I was directed to the back. I took a deep breath as the lottery began.

"Laban Team...Robyn Keisha Allard."

A curly-haired African American girl went to the stage, twisting her hands.

"Aleixo Filipe Romao."

A Portuguese teenager got up, his expression blank.

"Albern Darnell Ellis."

Al slowly went up to the stage, standing with other two Laban contestants. Lois reached into the girls' bowl again.

"Abagail Caroline Ellis."

My self-control broke and I buried my face in my hands, unable to look at the stage. I raised my head and caught the sadistic gleam in Lois's eyes as she seemed to look across the room at me. I knew deep down that she and Martha had planned this. I clenched my fists, finally understanding why I had been shown that video.

"Team Laban and Team Phineas… Circus Labyrinthos."

I forced myself to clap along with the rest of the audience, already knowing what I had to do. Gabby shot me a worried look as she slid her arm around Al's shoulders, following their team out the door. I stayed until they vanished down the hallway, my mind racing.

Back at my apartment, I told Davan what happened.

"We should have left." Davan's jaw clenched.

"Yes, we should have."

"It's too late for that now. Davan, I can't. We should have, but we didn't, and I am not letting this happen."

"What are you going to do?"

"Well, I know Gabby's probably going to tell Mom. I don't know what I can do."

I lifted the arm with the bracelet, wanting more than anything to scream. Davan took my hand, squeezing it reassuringly.

"I remember, the guards like the bathhouse on my floor. I could trap them in there."

"Okay. And what about this bracelet thing?"

"I bet Martha's got a way to take it off."

His shoulders sagged.

"I know this isn't much of a plan, but it's the best shot we're going to get. Hell, probably the only shot we're going to get."

A voice from behind made me jump.

"You two almost finished?"

"Yeah." Davan stood up, me on his heels.

As the guard left for the night, I seized my chance and dialed my home address. Mom's face popped up, asking what was going on.

"Why haven't we heard from you? Are you two all right?"

"I'm fine, Mom. I got in trouble with Martha. We've been under house arrest. They put this thing on me, and I can't leave. But listen, I need you to do something for me. Al and Gabby, they've both been chosen."

Rage and sorrow burned in her eyes. "Gabby told me. She told me about Martha too."

"Mom, I think it's my fault."

"Now honey, don't –"

"Mom, I broke the rules. In the Circus, I helped the other team."

"They would have died otherwise, I'm sure. Sweetie, you did what anyone would have done. I don't blame you."

"Thank you, Mom."

"Is there a way to take that bracelet off?"

"I don't know."

"Just...hang in there, okay?" Mom's eyes brimmed with tears. "Your dad or I will come get you."

"And then?"

"And then we're leaving. I've heard it all, Dawnielle. There's a war coming."

I felt cold and painfully aware that my old life was over for good.

"I love you, Mom. Tell Dad and everybody for me." I ducked my head as I started to cry.

"I love you too, Dawnielle. And I'm so proud of what you did."

She smiled briefly, her eyes bright and watery, and then the screen went dark. Mom's last words kept me awake for hours as I stared at the ceiling, unable to think of anything but what the next day would bring.

ABOUT THE AUTHOR

Tessa Rice graduated from West Hawai'i Community College and has attended several writing groups & workshops in order to pursue her writing career. Her positive outlook and approach to living with Asperger's Syndrome is nothing short of remarkable, leading her to her first major work, *Eternus*. Her passion lies with writing science fiction, mostly dystopian/superhero, two genres that inspired her to start her own trilogy.

She lives in sunny Kailua-Kona on the Big Island of Hawai'i.

KRG Publishing specializes in paperback, hardback and eBook publishing with a focus on Metaphysical, Esoteric, Paranormal, Hawaiiana and Educational genres. Take your first steps to a successful writing career at www.KahunaResearchGroup.org/publishing.

We offer some of the highest royalties in the USA!
$0 up front costs* **(*complete ebook manuscripts)**

Hawai'i: (808) 238-2264
Email: publisher@kahunaresearchgroup.org

Experience Supernatural Hawaii
• Ghost Tours
• Vortex Tours
• Other Activities
• Hawaiian Weapons
• Cultural Crafts
• Research Services
• DVDs & Books
Big Island
Ghost Tours
(808) 238-2264
BigIslandGhostTours.com
Find us on
Facebook
tripadvisor

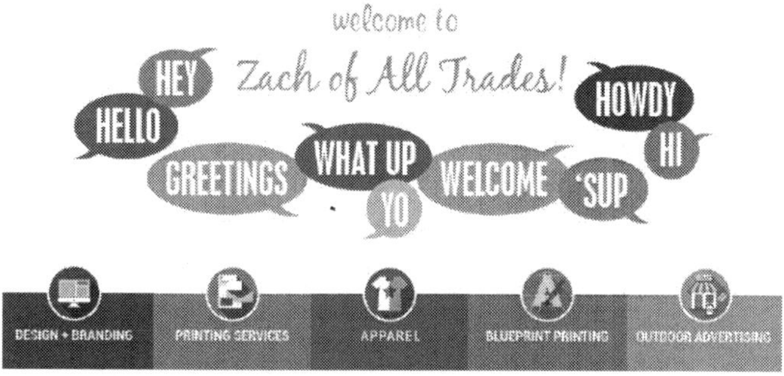

Web design, publishing & more at ZOAT.org.

Made in the USA
Columbia, SC
31 March 2022

58237278R00050